T0197529

# The Hand-Me-Down Dragon Boy Shirt

by Victoria Aranda

illustrations by Hilbert Bermejo

**To order additional copies of this book, contact:**
Xlibris Corporation
1-888-795-4274
www.Xlibris.com
Orders@Xlibris.com

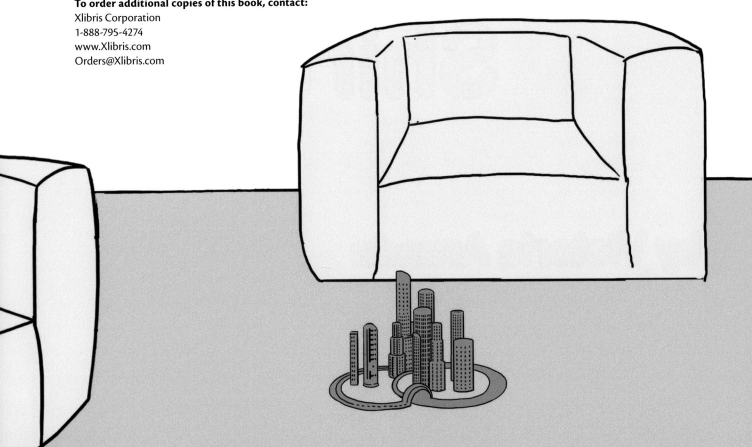

This book is for Shane,
Roman, and Baron—
the generous boys of
the hand-me-down
Dragon Boy Shirt.

V.A.

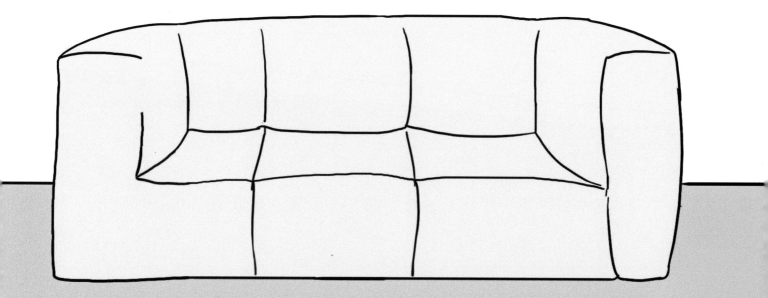

Ben has a shirt that is so special
he wants to wear it
**every day
for the rest of his life.**
He got it from the cool kid next door
in a bag of secondhand clothes.

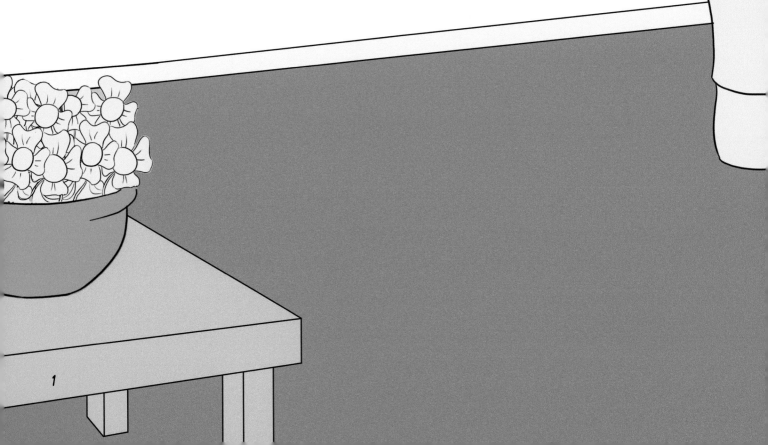

1

2

He likes the Dragon on the front,

the fire-red color,

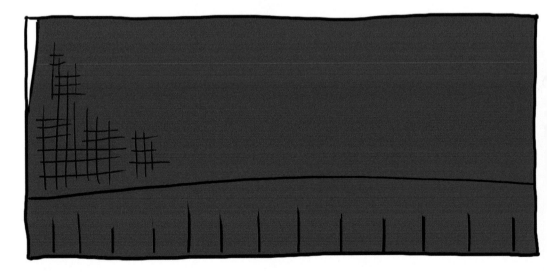

and the strong wings that catch air.

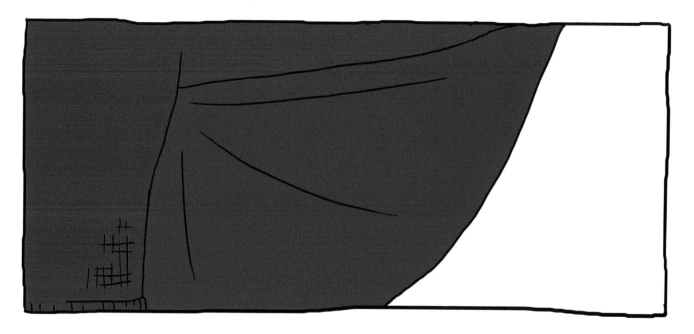

He likes that the shirt follows him everywhere.

Ben dodges crawlers as he runs
with his strong wings beating. "Watch me fly," he yells.
He stretches out his arms and the wings catch air.

5

Ben jumps.

Little brother says, "Wow, you fly! I want to fly too."
"You can't. Only one shirt."

Ben wears his shirt every day and every night.
There are times Mother wants to wash the shirt.
"Just for an hour. I'll help you keep watch,"
she says.

Ben lowers
his hand-me-down
Dragon Boy
sleeves and
sighs, **"Okay."**

Just then, little brother happily guesses, **"My turn."**
"No way. You rattle and circle little snake.

I move like a **Dragon**.
I have **fire** inside of me."

Ben's little brother says, "I have **fire** in me too."

At the park, Ben runs with his wings out laughing. A man walks up. He says, **"Stop.** Your boy looks happier than a tornado in Kansas. Where can I buy that great shirt?"

A boy runs up.

He says, **"Stop.** I want a shirt like yours too."

Ben smiles at everyone.
He holds out his arms.
He yells, "Watch me go,"
and his laughter fills the park.

Then he hears Mother explain.

"That hand-me-down shirt is really special. But, I'm afraid you won't find another one like it because it's too old. Right now it's Ben's favorite. When he outgrows it, it will go to his brother.

Isn't that right, Ben?                    Ben?"

But Ben has flown away.

Later on, Ben coughs.
He looks down at
the Dragon on the front.
"My arms are getting too big for you," he breathes.

**"That's
Impossible!"**

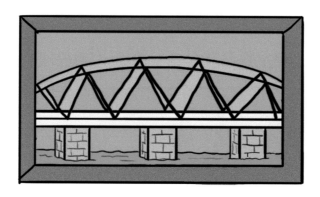

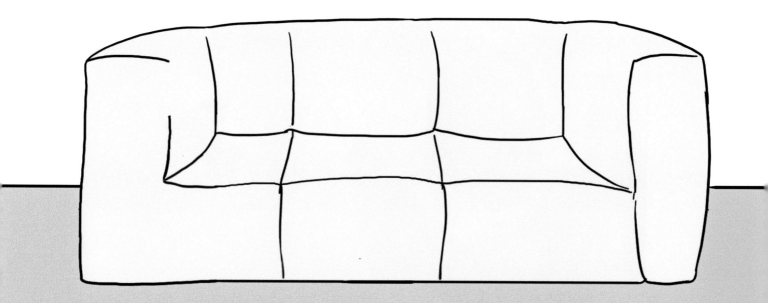

In the big room, Ben runs. He stretches out his arms.
He jumps. He flies away.

As he soars, he sees his little brother

stuck, circling the floor.

**"Stop."**
Ben spreads out his arms to catch the little crawler.

Brother holds out his hand, smiling. **"My turn?"**

Ben thinks of flying high. "Higher than anything,"
he whispers. He lowers his hand-me-down
Dragon Boy sleeves and says, **"Okay."**
He takes hold of his brother and stares him in the eyes.
"Come on, you better be ready for this.
You're gonna learn how to fly.
Someday soon, you'll learn the ways of

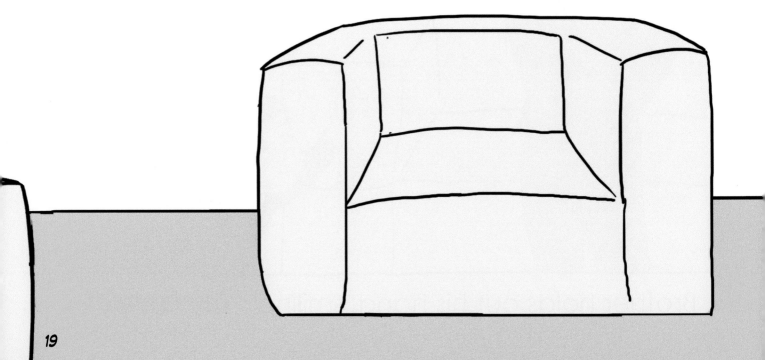

# the Dragon."

Printed in the United States
by Baker & Taylor Publisher Services